STEPPING STONE STORIES

A Funeral For Whiskers

by Dr. Lawrence Balter

UNDERSTANDING DEATH

Illustrated by Roz Schanzer

BARRON'S

New York • London • Toronto • Sydney

All inquiries should be addressed to:
Barron's Educational Series, Inc.
250 Wireless Boulevard
Hauppauge, NY 11788

International Standard Book No. 0-8120-6153-5

Library of Congress Catalog No. 91-391

Library of Congress Cataloging-in-Publication Data

Balter, Lawrence.
   A funeral for Whiskers : understanding death / by Lawrence Balter;
illustrated by Roz Schanzer.
         p.   cm. — (Stepping stone stories)
   Summary: Sandy is very sad and upset when her cat Whiskers dies,
but her parents help her understand and accept the loss.
   ISBN 0-8120-6153-5
   [1. Death—Fiction.   2. Cats—Fiction]   I. Schanzer, Rosalyn, ill.
II. Title.   III. Series.
PZ7.B2139Fu   1991
[E]—dc20   91-391
                                                              CIP
                                                               AC

PRINTED IN HONG KONG

1234   4900   987654321

CELEBRATION LUTHERAN CHURCH
931 N. 5th Ave.
Sartell, MN 56377

Dear Parents and Teachers:

The books in this series were written to help young children better understand their own feelings and the feelings of others. It is hoped that by hearing these stories, or by reading them, children will see that they are not alone with their worries. They should also learn that there are constructive ways to deal with potentially disrupting circumstances.

All too often children's feelings are brushed aside by adults. Sometimes, because we want to protect youngsters and keep them happy, we inadvertently trivialize their concerns. But it is essential that we identify their emotions and understand their concerns before setting out to change things.

Children, of course, are more likely to act on their feelings than to reflect on them. After all, reflection requires tolerance that, in turn, calls for a degree of maturity. A first step, however, is learning to label and to talk about one's feelings.

I also hope to convey to parents and others who care for children that while some of a child's reactions may be troublesome, in all likelihood they are the normal by-products of some difficult situation with which the child is trying to cope. This is why children deserve our loving and patient guidance during their often painful and confusing journey toward adulthood.

Obviously, books can do only so much toward promoting self-understanding and problem-solving. I hope these stories will provide at least a helpful point of departure.

Lawrence Balter, Ph.D.

It was a Wednesday morning not too terribly long ago in the town of Crescent Canyon, and Sandy Adams was getting ready for school.

"C'mon Whiskers," said Sandy. "It's time to get dressed."
Sandy's cat Whiskers was old, and she needed two tries before
finally landing squarely on Sandy's bed.
"You ready?" called Sandy's dad.
"Not yet," answered Sandy. "Whiskers needs to finish dressing."
Whiskers allowed Sandy to put a ribbon on her, but the old cat
was just not very playful this morning.

After dressing, Sandy went downstairs to feed Whiskers.
"I can't find Whiskers' bowl," she said.
"Just take any dish from the cupboard for now," answered
her mother. "I'll look around for her regular bowl while you're
in school."

"Here's some delicious breakfast," said Sandy,
spooning Whiskers' favorite chunky tuna into a saucer.
Whiskers just curled up next to the dish.
"And here's some yummy breakfast for you, young lady," said
Sandy's mother. "Let's get a move on."
Sandy drank her juice and munched her cereal, but Whiskers
didn't touch a bite of her food.
"Mom," said Sandy, "how come Whiskers isn't eating
anything? Do you think she wants some of my cereal?"

"Maybe Whiskers is just taking a lot of time waking up this morning," answered her mother. "Now I hear your school bus, so hurry up. Call upstairs to Dad, and give me a kiss good-bye." Whiskers didn't follow Sandy to the door or climb up to the window to watch her leave.

After Sandy had left for school, her mother took a long look
at Whiskers.
"There is something wrong with you today, isn't there?" she said.
She gathered up the old cat in her arms and tickled her chin.
"I think this calls for a trip to the vet."

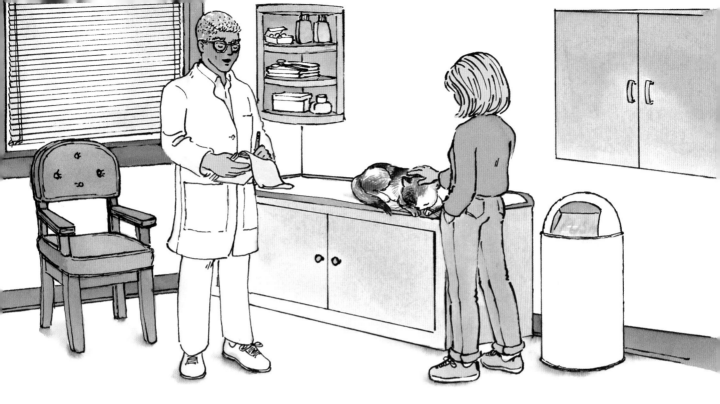

Dr. Perkins looked serious as he examined Whiskers.
"You'll have to leave Whiskers here with me for the day," he said.
"I want to do a few tests and examine her some more."
"What do you think?" asked Sandy's mom nervously.
"Well, Marge, it may be her heart and lungs," Dr. Perkins said.
"And she's quite old, you know."
"Please do all you can," said Sandy's mom. "You know how much
we all love Whiskers."
"Of course. Try not to worry," he said. "I'll call you later, when I
know more."

Later, when school was out, Sue Lee and Alfred came home with Sandy.

"Hi, kids," greeted Sandy's mom. "Want a snack?"

"Where's Whiskers?" asked Sue Lee.

"Here kitty, kitty," called Sandy. "Come here, Whiskers."

No Whiskers.

"Where's Whiskers?" asked Sandy in a nervous voice.

"I took her to the vet while you were at school," said her mom.
"My dog got his shots at the vet," said Alfred. "Is Whiskers getting shots, too?"
"She wasn't looking well this morning," explained Sandy's mom.
"Why didn't she come home from the vet's?" asked Sandy.
"Dr. Perkins is examining her to see what's wrong," answered her mother.
The kids played together for the rest of the afternoon, but Sandy's mind was on Whiskers.

At dinner that evening, the whole family was there except
Whiskers.

"I'm worried about Whiskers," said Sandy's mom. "She just didn't
look right this morning."

"What did Dr. Perkins think?" asked Dad.

"He needed to do some more tests," she answered. "And he said
he'd call to let us know."

Sandy put down her fork and stopped chewing. "Will Whiskers get
better?" she asked.

"I don't know," answered her mom in a serious voice. "I hope so."

Just then, the phone rang.

"Hello?" answered Sandy's mom. "Yes. Yes. I see. Oh, no!" Sandy's mom sat down.

"Thank you for the call, Dr. Perkins," she said in a quavery voice. "Good-bye."

When she hung up the phone there were tears in her eyes.

"What did he say about Whiskers?" Sandy asked quickly.

Sandy's mother reached over to hold her hand.

"Oh, sweetie," she said sadly, "he said that Whiskers was very old and very sick, and even his best medicines couldn't help her. Our poor lovely Whiskers has died."

Sandy felt as though she had a lump in her throat.

Nobody felt much like finishing dinner.

While Dad cleared the table, Sandy sat with her mom on the couch.

"I don't want Whiskers to be dead," said Sandy sadly.

Her mother squeezed Sandy tightly to her.

"I know what you mean," she said softly. "Whiskers was here when I brought you home from the hospital."

A tear rolled down her mom's cheek.

They snuggled closer still, and quietly held each other for a long while until it got very late.

"We'd better get you ready for bed," her mother finally whispered. "It's late, and it's been a sad day. We could all use a good night's sleep."

After she had washed and brushed her teeth, Mom and Dad joined Sandy in her bedroom.

"I want Whiskers to cuddle up in my bed, like always," said Sandy.

"I'm afraid she can't do that anymore, dear," explained Dad.

"YES," demanded Sandy. "I NEED HER TO."

"I'll sit here for a while to help you fall asleep," suggested her mom softly.

After a long while, Sandy finally fell asleep.

The next morning, everyone seemed to move around the kitchen a little more slowly than usual.

"Where is Whiskers, anyway?" demanded Sandy.

"At Dr. Perkins' office. After breakfast Dad's going to bring her body home in a special box," her mom answered softly.

"I called work and told them I'd be a little late this morning," said Dad. "I'd better get started."

"Can I go, too?" asked Sandy.

"I'd rather you stay here with me," answered her mom. "I think we ought to draw some pictures and make some ribbons for the box and...get ready for the funeral."

After breakfast, Sandy and her mom got out some tissue paper and markers and ribbons and made decorations.

In a way, it was like for a party, Sandy thought.

"What's a funeral?" she asked, as she tied another bow.

"It's a time when we say good-bye to someone who has died," explained her mom. "When we bury them and remember nice things about them."

"But I don't want to say good-bye to Whiskers," objected Sandy. "I want to play with her."

"She can't play anymore," explained her mom, "because she's dead."

"What's it like to be dead?" asked Sandy.

"Remember when you found the dead bird in the backyard? He couldn't fly anymore," her mother began. "Well, Whiskers can't purr or climb or play anymore."

"But Whiskers is mine. She can't get dead," protested Sandy. "I want her to come back."

"When something is dead," explained her mom, "it can't come back."

Sandy got a sad feeling when she thought that she would never be able to play with Whiskers again.

CRESCENT CANYON
YELLOW PAGES

"But you said Dad was going to bring Whiskers home from the
vet's," reminded Sandy.
"Yes. Dad's bringing her body home so we can hold a funeral for
her," explained her mom. "But it's just her body because she isn't
alive anymore."
Just then they heard Dad's car come up the driveway.
He looked very sad as he walked into the house carrying a large
box in his arms.

"We've made some pretty decorations for the box," said Mom.
"Let's pick a nice place in the yard to bury her," suggested
Sandy's dad.
"But won't she be scared to be buried all alone outside?"
worried Sandy.
"She won't mind," assured her mom. "When you're dead you don't
feel lonely or scared."

"Why can't we keep her in my room?" asked Sandy. "Then she won't miss me."

"She can't miss you," explained her mother. "But we're alive, and we can feel sad and miss someone who's dead."

"What's going to happen to Whiskers, now?" asked Sandy.

"When someone dies we usually bury them in a cemetery," said her mom. "And you can keep her alive in your mind by thinking about the things you used to do together."

They went outside and picked a spot to bury Whiskers.
"Let's dig a grave over here next to the flowers," suggested her mom. "It's a peaceful place."
Dad dug a hole in the soil with his shovel.
When he was finished, he gently placed the box in the hole.
"Good-bye," whispered Dad.
"Good-bye, sweet Whiskers," said Mom.
On the box she placed the little rubber spider that Whiskers had always loved to play with.
"Good-bye, Whiskers," Sandy said, brushing away a tear.
She put in a picture she had drawn.
Then Dad covered everything with earth.

"What are we going to do with Whiskers' bowl and her toys?"
asked Sandy when they came inside.
"Let's keep them for a while," said her mom. "Then we can decide."
"I've got to get to work now," said Dad. "I'll see you later."
He kissed them both and left.

"Is Daddy going to die?" asked Sandy suddenly.

"Don't worry," said her mom. "Daddy is young and healthy. He'll be here with us for a long, long time. Whiskers was very, very old and sick."

"Is Grandma going to die?" asked Sandy. "She's old."

"She is getting older, but she's healthy. I don't think she'll die soon," explained her mom. "But all living things die someday. The leaves on the trees die, and the flowers, the fish and the gerbil at school. Even people."

"Will you die?" asked Sandy.

"Not for a long time," said Mom as she hugged Sandy tight.

"Who will take care of me when you die?" asked Sandy.
"By that time, you'll be all grown up and probably be taking care of your own children," she said. "You won't need me to take care of you."
"I don't want you to die, ever," said Sandy very seriously.
"I plan on being around for a long time," her mother said with a smile.

"I wish Whiskers would come home," said Sandy.
"It hurts when someone we love goes away," agreed her mom.
"But we can remember all the nice times we used to have
with Whiskers."
"Do you think she'll come back if I find her bowl and don't make
her wear a ribbon?" asked Sandy sadly.
"You didn't do anything to make her die," Sandy's mom said,
hugging her. "It's just that she was very sick. The doctor tried to
make her well, but even he couldn't."

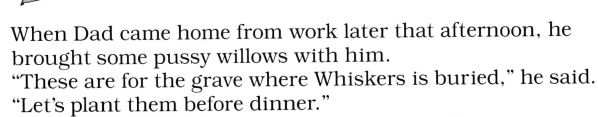

When Dad came home from work later that afternoon, he
brought some pussy willows with him.
"These are for the grave where Whiskers is buried," he said.
"Let's plant them before dinner."
Sandy and Mom helped Dad set the pussy willows in an
even row in the backyard.

After dinner they all went up to Sandy's room.

"Let's hang up some photographs of Whiskers on your wall," suggested her mom. "That way you'll always be able to remember her."

Sandy and her mom and dad stayed up really late looking at all their pictures of Whiskers and talking about her.

"Prrr, prrr," Sandy imitated the sound Whiskers made when she brushed her coat.

Mom and Dad and Sandy laughed and cried together as they remembered all the funny things they loved about Whiskers.

The next day, Sandy missed Whiskers as soon as she woke up.
She got an empty feeling inside when she realized that Whiskers
would not be there ever again.
Before she left for school, Sandy sat down on the living room rug
where Whiskers always loved to snuggle up.
Then she saw it behind the couch.
"I found Whiskers' bowl," Sandy announced happily.
"I'm so glad," said her mom. "And it's good to see a smile on your
face, sweetheart. It's been such a sad time."

Outside, on her way to meet the school bus, Sandy
stopped to look at the pussy willows they had planted.
The sun streamed down on that spot of earth.
The pussy willows were young and healthy and would
someday become big and strong.
Sandy thought of Whiskers.
Suddenly, she ran inside the house.

When she came out she had Whiskers' bowl
under her arm.
"I'm going to take it to school and give it to Hortense, our
rabbit," Sandy said proudly. "She needs a new one."
"I think Whiskers would like that," said her mother. She
gave Sandy a big hug.

The sun was warm that morning in Crescent Canyon, and it filled
Sandy with feelings of hope.
It would take time for the healing to happen.
But it would happen in time.
Sandy smiled and waved good-bye as she stepped on the bus.